35706

DATE DUE

MAKING TRACKS

by Adrienne Wolfert

Illustrated by Justin Bell

SILVER MOON PRESS
NEW YORK

First Silver Moon Press Edition 2000
Copyright © 2000 by Adrienne Wolfert
Illustrations copyright © 2000 by Justin Bell
Edited by Judy Hoffman

The publisher would like to thank Ronald Schatz
of Wesleyan University
for historical fact checking.

For information:
Silver Moon Press
New York, NY
(800) 874–3320

Library of Congress Cataloging-in-Publication Data

Wolfert, Adrienne.
  Making tracks / by Adrienne Wolfert ; illustrated by Justin Bell.
    p. cm. -- (Adventures in America)
  Summary: In 1934, in the midst of the Depression, fourteen-year-old Harry James
Harmony runs away to find his father who has traveled to Chicago in search of work.
  ISBN 1-893110-16-8.
    1. Depressions--1929--Juvenile fiction. [1. Depressions--1929--Fiction. 2.
  Runaways--Fiction. 3. Fathers and sons--Fiction.] I. Bell, Justin, ill. II. Title. III.
Series.

PZ7.W82114 Mak 2000
[Fic]--dc21

                                                                    00-022441

10 9 8 7 6 5 4 3 2 1
Printed in the USA

To Judda and Julius Wolfert
who always had time to listen

— AW

ONE

HARRY JAMES HARMONY BACKED INTO A corner and slid down against the wooden boards. He held the burlap sack with all his belongings tight between his knees. Beneath him, the earth shook so hard, his teeth chattered. But it was only the friction of the train wheels gathering speed and the couplings that joined the freight cars together.

He had done it. He had actually run away!

Bridgeport, Connecticut sped by. Its ships in the harbor, its smokestacks and oil tanks, its spires and chimneys, were misty in the steam from the engine.

Harry would never have made the train if it weren't for the man with the derby hat. When Harry raced for the train, he'd heard the shout "Grab on!" He lunged at the rough brown hand that was offered to him. Although the man's derby hat and baggy pants reminded Harry of Charlie Chaplin, the funny little man in the movies, the old guy was strong enough to pull Harry up like a sack of potatoes. Harry was fourteen-years old. The man's derby hat didn't even fall off his head.

As his eyes grew accustomed to the dark, Harry

saw that he and the black man with the derby were not the only ones in the box car. There was movement from what appeared to be a heap of rags piled on the rattling floor.

Derby's face flashed in a wide grin. He spoke to the raggedy heap. "Well, how there, Trip Ahoy?"

A hoarse voice replied, "Thought you was in Kansas City."

"Trip Ahoy's traveled over fifty thousand miles and never been picked up by the cops," Derby explained to Harry over the noise that had settled into a chug-a-lug rhythm.

"Runaway?" the hoarse voice barked, waving an arm toward Harry.

"Running to," Harry James said, "Running to my Dad." The car was full of shadows turning into people.

"This here's Poke," Derby nudged Harry and pointed to a boy Harry's age lying on the floor. His hair was so light, it shone in the dark. He didn't move.

The box car smelled of old wood, sweat, and coal gas. Some of the men knew each other. They greeted Derby with head nods and grunts.

"Looking for work?" asked one of the heaps. "This train's going to Pennsylvania Station in New York City, the world's largest city."

"Not the same," Derby said, removing several layers of shirts and sweaters. He wasn't a roly-poly man at all. "New York used to be good for kids and coloreds. You could get tips carrying luggage. Now

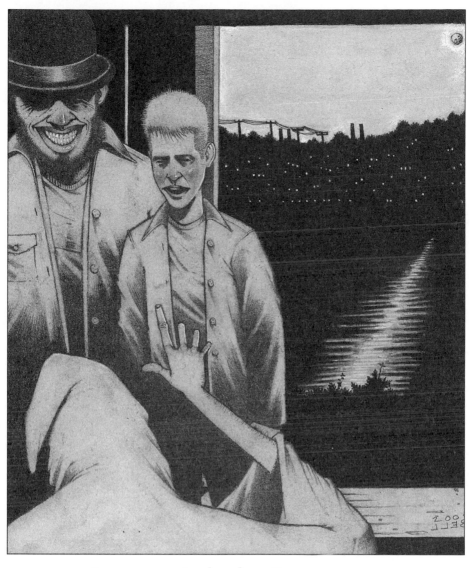

you can't even get in the door."

Harry's dad had black friends. He said that black people should join unions and that all people had a right to decent wages and permanent work. Otherwise, it was dog-eat-dog.

His dad also said it was wrong that their colored friends could not eat or sleep in the same hotels as whites. Often, they slept on the bus. Harry's father was upset by things that he thought weren't fair.

So was Harry. That's why he ran away from a really good foster home.

"Get to Chicago. They're hiring in the stock-yards," said Trip Ahoy in his rusty voice.

"I been working on a farm all summer," Harry said. He'd be having fresh baked huckleberry pie if he were still on the farm. Harry felt a pang of hunger, thinking of the food in his burlap sack.

As though he knew what Harry was thinking, Derby said low enough so that the others couldn't hear, "Whatever you got in that bag, eat it or put it on."

"Sure," Harry said, but thought, *I'll save it for later*.

Everyone gave up talking and listened to the rails. Derby curled up on his clothes. Harry closed his eyes. The noise diminished to a cymbal of steady clacks.

Harry's dad had taught him to play the piano. Songs went around with the wheels in Harry's head. Especially the one he had learned first.

"Grab your coat" . . . clickety . . . "and get your hat" . . . clack . . . "Life . . . " click "Can be so sweet . . . " clickety clack . . . . He blended the rhythm of the songs to fit in with the rhythm of the wheels. He was used to sleeping with noise. Noise had been his lulla-by since he was a baby living in the city. His father practiced till neighbors hollered. Sirens and horns seemed to sound all night. The farm he'd just left often seemed too quiet for him.

Better not tell anyone he had money in his shoe—that he didn't need to work right away—he thought as he fell asleep. He figured he had enough for meals until he reached Chicago, and then he'd find his dad. He was old enough to take care of himself.

Even in his sleep, he heard the noise, and it blended in with the dream he had of being together again with his family the way they'd been before mom got tuberculosis and had to go to the sanitarium. They'd lived in the little apartment, mom and dad sleeping in the one bedroom, and Harry on the couch opposite the piano. When he was little, he thought of the dark hulk of the piano as some friendly elephant—hovering over his sleep. Maybe because the black lacquer on the piano was cracked like a tough hide, maybe because the keys were made of ivory, like the tusks of an elephant. Dad always answered questions about how he made a living by saying, "W-e-l-l, I tickle the ivories!"

"Sure," Harry mumbled, and then he seemed to tumble over and over into a dark hole. Over and over. The music goes round and round, clickety-clack. Round and round.

His burlap bag slipped softly away.

"Hey!"

The towhead crouched in a little crack of light. Poke—backing away with all of Harry's belongings. Harry, with a shout, stumbled to his feet and started after him. Poke turned. He shoved Harry back. They wrestled.

The train whistle blew a loud, long toot.

Poke let go of Harry, thrust open the door enough to squeeze out, and jumped from the moving train. Harry leapt after him. He landed on his shoulder and rolled over. Cold, fear, air, and a shock ran through his body. He lay stunned in the long scratchy grass as the sound of the train grew more and more distant.

TWO

HARRY LIFTED HIS HEAD SLOWLY TO stare into Poke's eyes. Poke was getting up without trouble. *He's going to run away*, Harry thought, but, instead, Poke held out his hand. "You crazy fool," Poke said, helping Harry stand up. "You could kill yourself."

"Wh-what?" Harry sat up feeling dizzy.

"Are you okay?" Poke leapt up and peered down at him. Poke's face was round and freckled and he was just sprouting a moustache white as his hair.

"I-I guess so," said Harry, slowly getting up. He brushed the dirt off his dungarees. The brand new shoes, which the social worker had bought him for school, were scuffed.

"You better know about trains if you're going to ride them," said Poke. "I knew the train was slowing down because of the long toot. You don't just walk off, either, you look for a soft spot to land. These old boxes can run fifty miles an hour."

Poke picked up the bag. "Here's your stuff. I didn't want it anyway." He threw Harry's bag back at him and started off.

"Wait a minute," Harry said. "I've got some bread and fruit in there. You want to share it with me?"

Poke stopped short. "You're not mad?"

"Forget it," said Harry.

The two boys sat down at the railroad track, and Harry unwrapped the ketchup sandwiches he'd saved.

"Why do they call you Poke?" he asked.

Poke shrugged. "When I was a little kid, they used to say I was a poke all the time, so I thought it was my name. Your name is Harry, ain't it?"

"My dad named me after his best friend, Harry James."

"Who's he?"

"He's a trumpet player. My dad says he'll be famous someday."

When they finished eating, Harry carefully wrapped up the remaining food, which he saw was not much. It was the time of day when daylight and dark seemed to even out so it was neither. Even-ing, Harry thought, surprised. That's why they called it evening.

Poke led Harry along a length of rails that branched off the main track. "This here's a siding. At special times, a train will pull off and park here to let another train pass."

"You've jumped at sidings before?"

"In lots of places. This is my third trip," Poke said, rather proudly.

"Where are you heading?" Harry asked.

"Out West, maybe to Wyoming. I'm going to be a cowboy."

"Wyoming's further than Chicago. How long do you think it'll take you?"

"That's the next thing you better learn. It don't depend on distance. It depends on not getting caught. If you're under sixteen, the railroad police pick you up and put you in an orphanage. Or worse still, a reform school."

"That's why I ran away," said Harry.

"Well I turned sixteen this summer. You ain't fourteen, I bet."

"I guess I just turned sixteen this minute," said Harry. The wind had died down, the temperature had fallen with night. He shivered. He pulled his only extra sweater out of his bag.

Poke was looking over the landscape as though he owned it.

"See that?" Poke pointed to a faint white glow on the distant horizon. "We're going over there to sleep."

"What's that?"

"It's a fire. And where there's fire, it's warm." Poke was already striding through the weeds.

"But maybe it's a hobo jungle, and they're not friendly."

"Some are, some aren't," said Poke. Harry stumbled behind him. The ground was unfamiliar in the dark.

Pretty soon, they smelled the gases from the coal-fires. A few shanties were built on the field, some no more than cardboard boxes. Several fires were burning with coals probably scrounged from the railroad tracks. Figures huddled around each one. Harry smelled onions and burnt potatoes, which reminded him that he was still hungry. He was always hungry.

Harry stood close to Poke who seemed to know where they were and what they were doing there.

A pot suspended from forked sticks and a pole swung over one fire. A blanketed form was stirring something. Whatever it was, it would not be enough for all the people who were waiting to share it.

The two boys approached another group of three men sitting on the ground. "This here's a private party," growled the biggest one, lifting a wine bottle to his lips. "You git going, hear?"

A strong stench of sour wine hit Harry's nostrils. Poke pulled him away.

Turning, they nearly tripped over a clean-shaven man. Compared to the others he was well-dressed, that is, he was wearing a suit and overcoat. He was sitting on the ground, holding a felt fedora hat on his lap.

"Excuse me," Harry said, but the man stared blankly, his hands resting on the hat. The fingers were long and white, the nails clean.

A family had taken over the only real dwelling, an abandoned shed that was caved in on one side. They huddled in front of it. The father raked the coals to flame with a broken branch. The mother sat on an orange crate nursing a baby under her shawl. Two whimpering children crouched at her feet, heads in her lap. She shook her head sadly when the boys approached.

Harry quickly dug an apple from his bag. "Can I give it to them, ma'am?" He held it out to the children.

The woman examined him. She was quite beautiful. Like his mother, Harry thought.

The little boy reached for the apple, then looked at his mother. She nodded. He grabbed it and took a bite. His sister took a bite, too.

The man looked angry, "We don't need no charity."

"Maybe they do, Ed," said the mother. Then she turned to the children, a young boy and a girl around three or four. "Say thank you to the nice boys."

"Thank you," the children said politely.

"Sit down," the woman said. She looked at her husband. "They're just kids," she said. "How old are you?"

"Sixteen," Poke said quickly.

"Four—" Poke jabbed him in the side. Harry understood. "Sixteen."

"What else you got in that bag?" the little boy asked, coming closer to them.

Harry remembered that there was something in his pocket—the harmonica. It wasn't a real harmonica, but a toy prize from a box of candied popcorn. He worried for a moment that it might have fallen out when he jumped from the train, but no, it was still there.

The children watched him curiously. "I'll play you a song," Harry said. "But you got to sing it."

He breathed in and out of the harmonica to get the hang of it. He played "Mary had a little lamb" a bit off key. Not bad for a first try. The mother sang, and the children began to laugh and tried to follow her.

The baby looked out from under his mother's shawl. He was a thin pale-looking baby, but his eyes were bright.

"How about 'Jack and Jill'?"

The mother sang, " . . . went up the hill . . . "

She had a nice voice. Harry began slowly until he got the tune and then began to play faster. Dad always said that Harry had a good ear. He didn't need sheet music. If he heard a tune once or twice, he could play it.

The woman stood up and began swaying with the baby in her arms. The children held on to her skirt and jumped around. She wasn't a whole lot older than Poke.

*　　*　　*

They slept on the ground by the dying fire. All during the night, Harry dreamt about the farm he'd been living on this summer. He could hear a cow's plaintive wail, and he saw the cows. His favorite, Clementine, mooed again. His sleep grew pleasant with memories of the farm.

He remembered his first morning. The old farmer everyone called Pa woke him while it was still dark. "Cows can't wait," Pa said.

Ma made him sweet coffee, and they went out to the barn under the biggest, shiniest sky he'd ever seen. The stars hung so close, it seemed as though they perfumed the air. On the earth, the flowers and the vegetables lay like gifts.

At first Harry was afraid of the cows. They were so big. The biggest animal Harry had seen in the city was a policeman's horse, which had nothing to do with him. But there, on the farm, he found himself sitting on the little stool, head butted against a furry barrel, being told by the old farmer to tug on the teats. They felt rubbery and strange. Though he did what he was told, Harry didn't like the sensation at all. Not a drop of milk fell into the pail.

Suddenly the cow turned her head, looked at him, and let out a disapproving blast that knocked him right off the stool!

He felt the shock up his spine and heard the guffaws of the two hired men. They had no trouble at all getting a steady stream of milk as easily as turning on faucets. Of course, there were no faucets on the farm. Water had to be hand-pumped from the well.

Harry got up and brushed off his brand new overalls. They were bought for him by the State of Connecticut Child Welfare Department to wear at the Baron farm that summer of 1934.

Harry reached for the stool, but Pa Baron righted it first, which made Harry feel a little better.

"Now we got a problem," said Pa, putting his pipe in the pocket of his pants as though this problem would need two hands. "You just sit down here nice and easy and listen."

*   *   *

In the hobo jungle, Harry slept deeply and calmly all night. In his dreams he was in his attic room, on the rough clean sheets of his bed at the farm.

THREE

HARRY WOKE FEELING THE HARD ground beneath him. Poke whispered hoarsely into his ear, "Are you dead or what? Geez, I don't know how you slept like this with that crazy cow bawling since sun-up!"

Harry sat up, startled. For a moment, he didn't know if he had heard the mooing in his dream or in reality.

"Cow? A real cow?"

"You nuts? Of course, a real cow? Listen!"

No wonder he had dreamed about cows all night. A real cow was bawling in his ears. Harry thought again about that first day he had to milk a cow. "Do you know the song, O my darling Clementine?" Pa had asked that first morning when he was teaching Harry how to milk.

Harry sat down. Of course he knew that song. Since his dad was a musician, he knew about every song there was. Harry could play the piano too, and the first thing he liked about that farm was the piano he saw in the parlor. Maybe they'd let him play it.

But what did a song have to do with milking a cow? he wondered.

"Well this here cow's different from the others," Pa said, smoothing the rough red fur. "Daisy—over there—and Sue Ellen are Holsteins."

Of course they were different. Harry noticed that right away. The Holsteins were black and white, they were bigger than his cow by half and more ferocious looking. This cow looked like Elsie, the cow on the billboards that advertised milk. He'd never believed before that any real-life cow could look like that picture.

"She's a Jersey cow," Pa went on. "Her name is Clementine, and my daughter raised her from a calf."

Clementine pushed her head under his hand for further petting.

"She gives the creamiest milk of all, though she doesn't give as much as the others. My daughter always sang to her when she milked, and Clementine, here, won't give any milk at all unless you sing to her."

The barn became very quiet. The air was thick with hay and manure, and animal warmth. One little window let in the milky light of dawn.

So Harry sat down again and reached for the teats. He sang very softly, at first. The hired men stopped milking. The barn became quiet. Even the barn cats stopped mewing, and listened.

A thin stream of creamy milk rewarded his

efforts. So he sang louder, and the louder he sang, the thicker the stream flowed until the milk foamed up like a geyser from the silver pail.

"Hey, we got Bing Crosby here," one of the hired men called. At the mention of the famous crooner, everyone laughed.

*   *   *

Harry struggled to put his mind in order. He had awakened in a rough camp in a field. He was with his mom and dad. No, he was on the farm. No, he had run away from the farm.

Now he was in a hobo jungle. On the horizon, clouds purple with night paled to violet. Strings of smoke curled from the dying fires. The ground was strewn with bodies, asleep or simply unwilling to wake. It was like the scenes of foreign war refugees Harry had seen in the movies. Something heavy hung over the camp or perhaps rose from it.

They found a water bucket in the shed.

"Come on," said Harry. "Here, Bossy, easy now . . . "
"You hold her, Poke," Harry said, trying to maneuver the water bucket under the swollen udder.

"Me? Hold her? I ain't never seen a cow this close. She's Big!"

"She's a Holstein."

This meant nothing to Poke, who looked as pale as his towhead, even in the half-light. Gingerly he

reached for the furry body that was matted and full of burrs.

The cow was far bigger than Clementine. She stared at Harry through glazed eyes. She had probably strayed from her herd. She did not buck Harry; she just mooed. She was used to being milked by a farmer.

"Oh my darlin', oh my darlin' . . . " Harry coaxed.

"You're singing to a cow? You really are crazy, Harry!"

The cow kicked over the bucket. Harry picked it up.

"She's not stupid. She's hurting. She wants to be milked." He kept singing, stroking. "It won't hurt but a minute," he sang, as he gently touched the teat.

After they filled the bucket, they left the cow contentedly munching. Someone would be looking for her.

"We'll have to boil this milk," he said, as they carried back the full bucket between them.

"Why?"

"Don't you know you can get tuberculosis from unpasteurized milk?"

"No kidding. How do you know?"

"I know a lot about TB," Harry said sadly. "My mom has it."

But when Harry put the bucket of milk down beside the shed, Poke grabbed the dipper and took a long heavy drink.

"It's warm," he glowed. "And so good . . . " He had a real milk moustache.

Following Harry's warning, the mother boiled the milk and then invited the whole camp over to share it. Someone said that he had some rice, and he dumped the rice into the milk, which thickened it almost to rice pudding. The well-dressed man with the white hands refused at first but then, in the spirit of the gathering, accepted a bowl. Even the hoboes joined in, offering a bit of "spirit" for sweetener. The mother gently suggested they use it on their own portions.

FOUR

HARRY AND POKE WAITED IN THE LONG grass within sight of the water tower, a huge tank standing on a platform that raised it impressively.

"Why do they need so much water?" Harry asked.

"Water makes steam, dummy," Poke said. "And steam runs the engine. Do you know that one quart of water makes 1,760 quarts of steam? The old guy, Derby, told me."

"Oh, that's why they keep burning coal. So the water will boil and make the steam!"

Poke made a razzing sound. "Yeaaagh! The fireman will be so busy refilling tanks, he won't notice us sneaking aboard."

A couple of other rail riders walked stealthily from the "jungle." Now they hid in the grass far apart from each other.

"Just in case," Poke said.

"In case what?"

"Some of the railroad guys feel sorry for us and look the other way when we make the dash. The tough ones call the cops. In case a bum gets caught, the rest of us run like rabbits. They can't catch everybody."

Poke raised his head and scanned the field.

A rumble in the earth. Three whistles. The train chugged out of the distance, like a tired iron horse. It came to a noisy stop less than twenty yards from where the boys were hiding.

Harry got ready to run. Poke held him back.

A trainman appeared. He looked up and down the track. One hobo turned and ran away. The trainman folded his arms and stood guard while the fireman, with overalls, shirt, and face covered with soot, quickly climbed the tower.

A second tramp jumped on the caboose.

Poke whispered, "See that tank car?" He pointed to a capsule-shaped car that he explained was for carrying liquids.

"It has a ladder at the end. Climb up to the roof. There's a rail around the loading hatch you can hang onto. Then lie low."

An argument started on the caboose. The brakeman was pushing a tramp off the platform. A conductor ran over to help him.

The engineer and the fireman kept on filling the boilers.

At that moment, Poke gave the signal, "Now!"

The boys raced for the tank car. Harry's sweaty palms slipped on the brass railing. He clutched tightly and caught onto the ladder. Heart racing, he climbed as fast as he could. The train began to

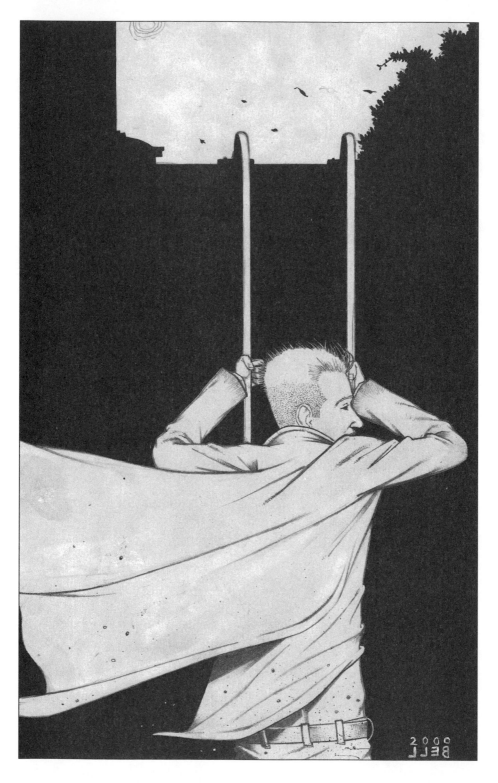

move. *I'm going to fly off this train and get killed,* Harry thought. But he flattened out and hung on for dear life.

Harry raised his head.

Poke was on the next compartment. "Darn!" he shouted into the wind. "We're next to the caboose."

"What does that mean?"

"Don't you know anything? The rear brakeman sits on top and watches the whole train. We have to take a chance going down the other way."

Poke turned his body around carefully. "Hurry, while we can still do it!" The wind blew the words out of his mouth.

Harry crawled after Poke to the ladder. It was harder getting down than up. The train was moving faster.

He was an insect clinging with a tiny part of himself to the side of the tank car, his jacket whipped into wings.

Poke jumped from the lower stair and disappeared. Harry didn't let himself think, put his feet together the way Poke told him and followed. For a moment, he soared over the speeding tracks, then hands and feet were gripping the door of the boxcar in panic. He fell into the darkness after Poke.

Harry lay where he fell a long time.

Everything was gone. The bag with the little food that was left, even the toy harmonica, had flown from his pocket.

All the strength was drained out of him. He knew for the first time what it was like to risk real death.

*   *   *

This box car was loaded with cartons, barrels, bundles, and crates. Harry and Poke made a hiding place among them. The cars might be searched.

Poke said, "I've run away every year since I was twelve. They picked me up once in New York, once in Chicago. I never made it farther than Chicago. But this time, I will make it. They can only put me in jail for vagrancy. That's a few days. And they have to catch me first."

FIVE

HARRY HAD RUN AWAY FROM THE FARM because he got into a fight with another boy. He knew that the social worker and the truant officer would be after him. They would take him away to reform school or some other place for problem children. Other children had told him about these "homes." Harry was not going into one of them. The last postcard he got from his dad had an address from Chicago, Illinois. Harry looked up Chicago on the map. It didn't seem so far. The quickest and cheapest way to get there would be by train. Maybe the only way without money.

When he got to Chicago he'd find his father.

Then they'd get his mother home from the sanitarium. He was old enough now to take care of her. He could even sell newspapers after school. They'd be together again, the three of them. On the sunny side of the street.

That was Harry's dream.

But this was not the adventure he had imagined. He certainly did not want to go into an orphanage. He didn't want to go to jail, either. Besides, it was taking longer than he planned. But, there was no going back, and going forward was all he could do.

Harry's dad, Ben, had promised to send for him as soon as he got settled somewhere. For now, Ben had to hit the road with the band. He didn't know where he'd be from one week to the next. Wherever they got a gig. The band wanted to end up in Hollywood, but they heard about unemployment lines with hundreds of musicians willing to take any job. A family man needed a steady job. The band would try Chicago, city of the blues. If they couldn't make it together, Ben would have to hire himself out solo. Play in bars and clubs. Work that could be steady.

Some day, mom would get better, and they would have an apartment again and Harry would have a home. Ben had ruffled his son's hair when he said that. Was it a promise or a dream? Harry wondered.

"But for now," his father said, "a kid is better off living with a family and going to school. I wouldn't be able to take care of you properly. It's only for a little while, son."

People said that Harry and his dad looked more like brothers than father and son. Harry was proud of his father's youthful looks, but Ben always frowned. "I'm your father," he said to Harry, "Don't forget that."

It was true that they resembled each other, but Harry's face was rounder and his eyes wider. Ben's hair was so curly, he plastered it down with hair gel, but Harry's was straight. A cowlick hung over one eye.

Harry's mother used to smooth it back. He could remember her doing that before she went away the first time. He was still little enough for Ben to take him along to rehearsals. The musicians called him their "mascot," and he sat on many different laps, getting instructions on every instrument in the band.

Dad said, "You and me, man to man, till mommy gets well."

When she did come back, mom said he mustn't kiss her. He might catch her sickness. They couldn't even eat off the same plates anymore. She had her special untouchable dishes.

When Harry looked sad, she sang him the introduction to their favorite song.

Walked with no one and talked with no one and I had nothing but shadows/then one morning you passed/and I brightened at last . . . .

They sang the chorus together, *Grab your coat and get your hat/leave your worries on the doorstep/just direct your feet/to the sunny side of the street . . .*

Some nights she went to work with Harry's dad.

That was how she had met his father. They called a girl singer "canary," and she was the canary in the band that Ben had formed, The Harmonies. Sometimes they entertained as a duet at some wedding or party.

"Don't, darling, you'll pull them out," she scolded, when Harry played with the fringe on the dress that she wore for those special occasions. The fringe swung around her legs when she moved. Dad wore his tuxedo. Harry thought they were the most beautiful people in the world.

Then one morning she woke up with a cold. She stayed in bed that day and the next, trying to cure herself for the gig that weekend. The morning after the gig, they were having breakfast when she began to cry. It seemed that she had coughed during one of her solos. She couldn't stop, and her hankie had blood on it.

"On the second phrase, imagine." Her eyes were teary and her cheeks very red.

"Mommy, you look like me when I have a fever," Harry said.

How many times had they quoted him on that sentence? *You look like me when I have a fever.*

"Five years old and he knew his mother was sick before she did. Or I did."

Her cough brought up blood, and she had to go away to rest at a tuberculosis sanitarium in Connecticut. She wasn't gone too long, but, as Harry grew older, his mother went away more often and for longer periods of time.

SIX

THE BOYS SLEPT FOR A LONG TIME. THEY woke in the night when the train stopped. Their car was uncoupled, backed up, and moved to another track. They lay fearfully, listening to the terrible clamoring. The car jolted backward and forward.

"What do you think is happening?" asked Harry.

"We're being sidetracked to another locomotive."

After what seemed hours of listening to train noises and men's shouting, they began to feel the wheels turn.

"I got a feeling we're not headed to New York anymore. We got to be lucky as to where we're going," Poke added.

"I'm hungry."

Poke found an old potato rolling around the floor, and they ate that and fell asleep again.

*   *   *

The train stopped at several stations. They heard men talking, and Poke said it sounded like they were unloading big cuts of ice from horse-drawn wagons. The horses were snuffling. Once in a while, a hurried searchlight swept past their hiding place. The train left the junction, the wheels began their rhythmic journey. Harry stared at the stale darkness counting the whistletops. There was nothing to do but remember.

*   *   *

It seemed forever since his dad had left him in Connecticut to find work in Chicago, a city known for its jazz and blues music. The social worker, Miss George, chose the first foster home in the same school district so Harry wouldn't have to change schools.

There were six kids in the house. Harry was just one more child in the pack.

Maybe it was easier for his father when they were separated. But Harry was unhappy. He wondered what kind of life his father was living now that he didn't have to worry about a kid.

When Harry came home from school, he put away his books and lay down on his bed. The other children ignored him.

In the morning, he didn't want to get up.

"Are you sick?" The foster mother felt his forehead. "You don't have a fever," she said, "Why are you acting sick? You can't get away with that in this house."

He had to do his chores and his homework. He

had to go to school. He had to play outdoors like the others. There was a lot of fighting. The foster parents fought. The kids fought each other.

There was no piano in the house. No radio. No singing. Harry didn't have a fever, but he felt very tired.

"What's wrong, Harry?" Miss George, the social worker, asked when she came to visit. "You're not doing so well in school."

He didn't know what was wrong. He felt resentful and lonely at the same time. There was no music in his head, only the hum of anger.

"You think your family abandoned you," Miss George said, "but that's not true. It's not your mother's fault that she's sick. And your father is trying to get a job. Your parents love you and want to be with you."

It was no one's fault. These were hard times.

"You mustn't brood about things that can't be helped."

*   *   *

The train slammed to a halt, then chugged along slowly. Harry peeked through a crack in the door.

"We're pulling up to a loading platform," Harry said.

"Holy Chee!" said Poke. "When did they put those icebox cars on?" They poked their heads out a little to see what was going on.

"I see some guys in butcher coats," said Harry.

"They're busy as bees." When they opened the box-car, frosty steam escaped.

The men wore thick sweaters and overalls under their coats. They marched slowly to the ice car. They lifted the quarters of beef off the hooks and swung them on their backs. The frost melted off the meat and onto their clothes.

"They must weigh two hundred pounds," Harry said. "We could make lunch money if we offer to help them."

"Can you lift two hundred pounds?"

"I don't know. How much does a pail of milk weigh?"

A horse-drawn wagon piled with large blocks of ice loaded from the icehouse pulled closer to the station.

The butchers lurched under their burdens.

Three trainmen ambled behind the loading platform and sat down on a patch of grass. They opened their lunch buckets and unwrapped thick sandwiches.

"I can smell salami all the way back here," said Harry.

One man took off his hat and opened his thermos. Another wiped his grimy face. Most certainly, he was the fireman.

"We gotta get off here. Take a chance they won't see us," said Poke. "When they're busy eating, slide down easy and walk as though you belong here."

Harry tried to imagine he belonged here,

wherever "here" was. He could see the telephone wires and chimneys of the main street as his feet hit the ground. There was a billboard on the side of the station that read, Barney's Restaurant and Bar, in thick black letters.

The loading men moved in a circle, piling the beef on the ice wagon, then returning for another load.

"Hello, boys." The train conductor looked suspiciously at them. Harry's instinct to run was so strong, his legs trembled from the effort to stop.

Poke said, easy as you please, "What kind of freight does this train carry, sir?"

"You boys interested in trains?"

"Yes, sir."

The conductor removed his cap. His gray hair had been flattened by the cap, and he smoothed it out.

"You name it and we carry it. From fruit to molasses. From Moxie to motor cars. This is locomotive 5477. A lucky number, don't you think?" He seemed very proud of his train.

The engineer stood up. He wore a neat uniform and cap. "Would you like to see how a train works? Most boys do." A long gold chain swooped across his chest to the large watch he pulled out of his pocket. "Come on, I've got time to show you."

He set down his lunchbox and motioned Harry to climb with him into the cab.

There was hardly room for three in the cab. Harry's foot slipped on a stray chunk of coal. He saw a bewildering array of handles, levers and gauges. The locomotive was hissing. He could feel heat from the firebox.

"You're standing where the fireman stands swinging his shovel of coal," the engineer said. "It's up to him to keep the fire going."

"What's that awful yellowish smoke?" Poke choked, coughing. "It's not just steam."

"It's from the oily rags, kindling, and firewood we use to start up the boiler. Some folks are saying it's unhealthy to breathe this stuff in all the time, but we don't even smell it anymore."

He disregarded Poke's choking sounds.

"You smell the oil in the cups and joints, too." He showed them oil cans, grease sticks, and his wrench. "I'm a train doctor too. Before we go out of the yard in the morning, I give the patient a good exam."

Poke's eyeballs rolled up with boredom. But Harry examined the throttle, wondering how the small instrument could control the power that moved this monster.

The engineer seemed very pleased to explain. "This is the pressure gauge for the steam. I check this gauge all the time to make sure there's enough air pressure in the system. The fireman has to shovel more coal if it gets low. He also injects the water through these pipes."

Harry looked back at the line of cars that snaked behind the locomotive, disappearing around the bend. "How do you stop all those cars at one time?" he wondered.

"Compressed air pipes run through the whole train. When I pull the vacuum brake-handle, it stops the wheels on every coach as well as the engine."

How must it feel to control all these cars with a grip of your own hand? How many cars were there . . . twenty? thirty?

"I'd like to blow the whistle," Poke said, pursing his lips and giving a good imitation of the train whistle.

"The whistles are not just for fun," the engineer said, as they rejoined the other men. "They're signals. Three short toots means stop. More than three means an animal or person is on the track. A long toot means rail crossing, tunnel, or station coming up."

"I know all that," Poke bragged.

"Did you ever hear the saying, 'blow off steam' when someone loses his temper?" the fireman asked, joining the conversation. He had soot smeared around his face. "Trains are where it comes from. A big tea kettle starts and stops the whole shebang."

"He blows off steam all day and night," the others laughed.

"You hear that lonesome sound at night? Think of us," said the conductor.

The boys looked at the men eating their sandwiches. They took large bites and chewed away happily. Ham and cheese, salami and pickle. The brakeman stuck a whole hard-boiled egg in his mouth.

"You kids want a sandwich?" one man asked. Poke and Harry didn't need urging. They attacked the food ravenously.

The men stopped laughing and looked at each other.

"How come you kids aren't in school?" the conductor asked, staring suddenly at the boys' soot stained clothing.

"Our school doesn't start until next week, sir!" Poke said quickly.

"We're in high school," Harry added. At least that wasn't a total lie. They were supposed to be in high school.

SEVEN

"NOW WHAT DO WE DO?" HARRY ASKED through a full mouth as they waved goodbye to the departing train. They were standing alone on the platform.

"Let's find out where we are, first." Poke stroked the short silky hairs on his upper lip, pretending they were a moustache. "If we're lucky, we'll be in New Jersey. Or maybe even Pennsylvania."

"We're not far from the depot," Harry said, "Let's walk over and wash up."

In the men's lavatory, Harry was shocked at the sight of himself in the mirror. What looked back at him was a soot-stained, rumpled ragamuffin. Poke looked better because his fine white hair did not get mussed. It fell back into place, naturally, but he was grimy, too. No wonder the conductor had looked at them funny.

They examined their bruises. Harry had a bad one on his shoulder. They washed with the harsh soap and wiped themselves with their shirts. Then they scrubbed their shirts, and Harry washed his socks. His dad was fussy about clean socks. But there was nothing they could do with the wet clothes except put them back on.

Harry took his money out of his shoe. "Let's get some supplies," he said.

Luckily, it was a warm day, and the shirts began to dry immediately. Harry's socks squished inside his shoes as they walked to town.

The main street was lined with clapboard stores faced with brick. Old foreclosure and going-out-of business signs hung crookedly in the windows. A line of scruffy, sad-looking men went from one open store to the other looking for work. Signs read NO HELP WANTED.

A few men stood on the porch in front of the general store, rolling cigarettes and handing them to each other. They watched Harry and Poke enter.

Inside the store, the boys spent a lot of time examining the items on the shelves. They argued about what they would buy if they had plenty of money. Finally, they picked out matches, biscuits, and a tin of sweet cocoa.

"Could we load your shelves or sweep your floor for this stuff?" Poke asked, setting it on the counter.

The clerk looked at them with a funny expression. "You two are my best customers so far today," he said.

Harry paid for the food, and the clerk tossed in the matches for free. "No hiring, today," he told the men on the porch.

They passed a hardware store. The owner's wife

shook her head. No work. A man was carrying boxes from her cellar. Probably for a meal.

A flashlight cost too much money, but Poke said a jackknife was a necessity. Harry doled out the money from his damp shoe. His shoes looked shabby even though he had cleaned them with toilet paper.

Harry looked longingly at a display of harmonicas.

An ordinary street of shops with displays of ordinary items of life seemed unreal . . . like a movie set. His head was muddled.

"If I had all the money in the world," Poke said, "I'd buy me a motor car. Then I'd drive to Wyoming."

"I'd buy me an airplane like Lindy's," Harry grinned. Charles Lindbergh was one of America's greatest heroes. Lindy was the first pilot to fly from New York to Paris. "I'd fly around the whole world."

He felt that it was possible.

*   *   *

The two boys roamed along the street. Ordinary people in ordinary clothes looked clean and well-fed. They wove in and out of the job-seekers and window-shoppers intent on their purpose. Harry stopped to examine the display of school clothes in the window of a department store.

"Who'd want to wear that sissy stuff?" Poke said scornfully.

"Absolutely No Hiring Today!!!" read the sign in the window.

Owners stood dejectedly in doorways. Harry peered into the darkened window of Barney's Restaurant and Bar. A song scratchily wavered from a console radio. A few men huddled over the bar. A man in spectacles and a woman in a red hat were sitting by the window table. Poke looked longingly at a plate of barbecued ribs she picked apart.

Partially hidden by a potted palm was an upright piano with cracked, yellowed keys.

As though drawn by a magnet, Harry walked right into the restaurant and up to the piano.

"Are you Barney?" Poke asked a man who wore a white apron with a large painted tiger over his stomach.

"Yep," said the man. His tie had the same tiger in miniature. "If you're looking for work, I just hired a dishwasher, and I got no more jobs. If you're hungry, there's a soup kitchen two blocks down that'll feed you."

The woman in the red hat put down her sandwich and watched Harry look longingly at the piano. "You play the piano?"

"Yes, ma'am."

"Go ahead, play something for us."

Harry looked back where Poke and Barney were talking.

"Go ahead," the woman said. Her lipstick matched her hat. "Hey, Barney, shut off the squeak box. This

kid's going to play 'Chopsticks' on your piano."

"Chopsticks" was a thump, thump tune every kid near a piano learned easily.

"It'll cost you a bottle of Moxie," the woman laughed.

"I'll take a cola," Poke said quickly.

"You got a heart of gold, Maribelle," said Barney. He switched off the radio.

"Nevermind about the cola," said Harry, "And I won't play 'Chopsticks'."

The piano stool was low enough to milk a cow. He wound it higher. The others watched him, including the men at the bar.

Harry closed his eyes. He used to beg his dad to let him play with the band.

He began, *Life can be so sweet/ on the sunny side of the street . . .*

The woman in the red hat sang, "Grab your coat . . . "

Harry played one chorus and stopped. Everybody clapped.

"Hey, you really tickle those ivories. Play some more."

Poke grabbed Harry. "No. We got to find a job," he said loudly and with a catch in his voice. "Our families are starving."

Barney pushed Poke aside "What else can you play?"

Harry sat down and played "When You're Smiling." The music brightened the dingy room, brought smiles to the adults' faces.

They began to sing, "when you're laughing/ the whole world laughs with you/ . . . "

People who were strolling by stopped in the doorway. Some kept time to the beat. Some of them sang along.

Two little girls started dancing. Their father ordered a couple of sodas.

Three men sat down at a table. "May as well eat lunch here. The music's nice."

"Just keep going," Poke said in Harry's ear. So Harry kept on going. *Toot, toot, tootsie, goodbye.* Everyone sang along to that. And then, "Sunny Side of the Street," again. Songs kept returning to him, songs he didn't know he knew. He hadn't played the piano since he left the farm where he played every day. He could feel his inside self singing and dancing through his fingers.

"You need a manager," Poke declared later. He had put an empty ash tray on the piano and was counting the change people had dropped into it. "Wow! We made almost a dollar!"

"You boys like some ribs?" Barney asked gruffly.

EIGHT

PEOPLE WITH TB HAD TO LIVE IN PURE clean air. They had to drink creamy milk and eat fresh vegetables to build up their health. They had to rest a lot to fight off the deadly germ.

That was why Harry's mom had to go to the TB sanitarium in northern Connecticut. It was a hospital that was also a large farm.

The sun was shining on the day Miss George brought Harry to the farm. It was June, and the fields were the new green of spring. The trees were dotted with crisp young leaves.

Harry liked the farm more than his first foster home, and he liked the idea that his mother was on a farm, too. He felt closer to her.

But he lied when people asked if she was in a sanitarium. TB was a contagious disease. People avoided the families of those who had it.

Except for poison ivy, Harry was never sick on the farm.

The work was hard. Along with hired men, he milked the cows, shoveled the barn, cleaned the stanchions, and scoured the pails. Then the gallons of milk had to be loaded on to the dairy's truck. Their work began and ended with daylight. The days began with Ma's blueberry pancakes and ended with her wonderful stews. Harry's favorite was the chocolate upside-down cake.

But there was work after supper, too. They weeded the garden in the cool of the evening. They filled their big pitchers with wash water for the commodes, and stumbled upstairs under the heavy weight. One night a week, they gathered around Pa's battery radio to listen to "The Lone Ranger" while they polished the sooty chimneys of the kerosene lamps. On Saturday evenings, Harry was permitted to hear "Your Hit Parade." He learned the top ten songs by ear and played them on the piano. On Sunday evenings, everybody eagerly awaited the Jack Benny program. Ma was always holding something on her lap, crocheting, socks, mending.

Otherwise, Pa saved his battery for the market reports in the morning and the evening news with Lowell Thomas.

Ma always said, "Goodnight, sleep well, Harry," before he went up to his room in the attic.

In the light of the kerosene lamp by his bed, he read *King Arthur And The Knights Of The Round Table*, which took him all summer to finish. He fell asleep, reading.

Harry's muscles hardened. He could lift things that he couldn't budge earlier in the summer. Pa said that he could see Harry outgrowing the corn.

Harry thought that his mom must be getting better, too.

But Ma and Pa were having a hard time paying for the farm. Milk prices were down, and they had to sell some cows. If they couldn't meet the mortgage payments, they would be foreclosed. The bank would take the house and the farm. They would lose their home. They looked more and more discouraged every day.

In the summers, a disease scourged the city, this one aimed at children. It was poliomyelitis, a sickness that paralyzed certain parts of the body. Almost every family had a member with a crippled leg or arm. If the child didn't die, he or she was doomed to be crippled for the rest of his or her life. There was one boy who lived in an "iron lung" that breathed for him. Only his head was exposed. When the news photographers took his picture, he was smiling.

Families from New York City would drive up in their jalopies looking for a place to escape polio. Many of the farmers rented room and board to the mothers and children. The fathers would come out on the weekends.

Someone recommended the Baron farm. One Sunday, the extra bedrooms in the house were rented to summer boarders.

That was when the trouble started.

*   *   *

At Barney's Restaurant and Bar, Harry played as long as the crowd stayed. He and Poke ate supper in the kitchen under the suspicious eyes of a sweating cook.

Afterward, Barney led them down to the storeroom in the basement. One wall was lined with shelves of beer and whiskey. Another was a honeycomb of wines. The third wall held cartons of canned goods and other supplies for the restaurant. Cases of soda were stacked on the floor. Barney pushed aside some empty boxes and cleared a space big enough for a couple of makeshift bedrolls.

"You kids can sleep down here tonight," he said. "And I don't want no mess. Don't touch nothing here."

He pointed to Harry. "You can play the piano afternoons for your keep. And you," he pointed to Poke, "you make yourself useful in the kitchen. You can keep any tips you get setting up and clearing the tables."

*   *   *

As they stretched out in the dark basement, Harry yawned. "It's nice lying here on something softer than the floor of a boxcar. I hope he lets us stay for a while."

He turned on his side to look at Poke who was lying beside him on the other roll of blankets. "How long since you slept in a real bed?"

"I'm never going to sleep on a real bed," said Poke. "Cowboys sleep on the range. You know that."

"They also sleep in bunk beds," said Harry, remembering a movie he'd seen. "They have a mattress and pillow and saddle blankets."

"When we leave here, we'll take our blankets. It gets cold in Chicago," Poke said.

"How can we do that? They're not ours."

Poke sat up. "Who says they're not ours? We work like palookas, and Barney doesn't pay us a cent. He owes us more than blankets!"

"But Poke, he could get grown men to work for food, too. Don't you know it's a depression?"

"Look who's telling me!" Poke was scornful. "You know how I lived the last three years I been running away? I go from hobo jungle to hobo jungle for something to eat. I seen hundreds and hundreds of down-and-outers. I seen guys jump in front of the train and kill themselves." Poke was a silhouette in the darkness. "I seen babies too weak to cry. I seen little kids in the tobacco fields and the bean fields picking vegetables from when they can see, to when they can't. You been living easy, Harry. Don't tell me it's a depression."

"Did you do that, Poke?"

"What?"

"Pick tobacco and vegetables twelve hours a day?"

"Fourteen in the summer. Six *a.m.* to eight *p.m.* My whole family did," Poke said.

"Where is your family?" Harry asked.

"I don't know. I got sent to reform school, and they had to go west with the crops. Last I know, they was heading for California." Poke lay back down, his hands under his head.

"I never went to school much," he said into the darkness. "We moved all the time, and the other kids were way ahead of us. They called us dummies and worse. I ain't lived in a real house since I was six years old. We lived in the car or in some crummy shack. I don't think I could sleep in a real bed."

The basement grew silent. Harry tried to think of something comforting to say to Poke.

In an afterthought, Poke changed the subject. "It'd be hard to steal from the old palooka," he said. "That tie has real tiger eyes."

*   *   *

A new kind of music brightened Barney's old console radio. It had a different beat from the regular songs of the Thirties. This beat fit in with the rhythm of the trains Harry rode.

Harry and his dad first heard jazz played in Harlem, but it never seemed the same when played anywhere else. The new music was faster than jazz.

Some big shot was quoted as saying that swing was dangerous. Its tempo was faster than seventy bars to the minute, faster than the human pulse.

But it seemed the right direction for Harry as he spent wonderful hours playing the piano in the afternoon. The song of the train had gotten into him. He could feel the screech of the wheels plowing the rails. He could hear the lonesome tone of the whistles—the couplings pulled apart just so far and together just so close, in a steady struggle.

His own voice made up a chant that raced ahead of the beat: the movement of stowaways jumping off trains, the bustle of commuters and trainmen shouting orders, the pace of men on the streets, a shuffle to join the long, weary breadlines, the steady cries of infants never fed enough.

All this came out of the air to Harry in a nervous beat for a stumbling earth. He had to drown out the old fears of the human race he saw around him. Working for nothing. Never going anywhere. The humdrum of life squeezed of its promise. You had to find another way, you had to jump, you had to soar, you had to scream, you had to whip your body into a wild frenzy of no, no, no, this isn't me!

NINE

"IT'S GOING TO TAKE FOREVER IF WE have to get to Chicago from here," Harry said. He was looking at a map of the United States. "We'll have to go South to go North, or East to go West. How much are you making on tips?"

"Not as much as you make playing the piano."

"Let's stay here until we make enough to buy tickets," said Harry.

"Tickets to where?" Poke asked.

"To Chicago. No one will be looking for us on a passenger train. Look, we've been here a week, and we have a lot of money already, don't we?"

Poke looked uncomfortable. "Yeah—three dollars and eighty-five cents." He lowered his voice, "Barney asked me twice if you're a runaway. He's getting suspicious."

"He's getting customers, too. I thought it was four dollars and eighty-five cents." Harry reached behind the cans of tomato soup where they kept the money from their tips. It was heavy with nickels.

"Yeah. Well—while you're having fun playing the piano, I'm peeling potatoes. I don't know how long I can stand this job." Poke looked crabby.

"One more week. We're eating and we have a place to sleep. We even got nice clothes from the Salvation Army." Harry stroked the wool parka the Salvation Army ladies had given him. Poke had picked out a leather army jacket from the Great War. "If we save every cent . . . "

"I put something in that box, too," Poke said.

Harry frowned. "You took something out, too."

"Fifteen cents for smokes."

"What about the movies? You went to see Tom Mix. And beer? You're too young to drink beer anyway."

"There's other things in life besides playing the piano, you know."

"Yeah," said Harry. "Like getting where we're going. Or don't you really care about getting to Wyoming?"

Poke glared at him, but didn't answer.

*   *   *

In the quiet of the storeroom, memories of the farm came rushing back to Harry.

For days before the boarders came from the city, their cars sagging with boxes and luggage, the farm had been in upheaval. Harry was sent from the barn to help Ma and the other foster child, a girl named Maggie, move beds and dressers, scrub floors, air rugs, unpack dishes, empty closets, make beds, polish windows, dust, sweep, and set up the summer kitchen on the porch.

These things were not easily done when they had to pump water and heat it on the old iron stove for washing and mopping.

That job fell mostly to Harry.

"Whew!" Ma said, her face flushed and covered with perspiration.

She didn't stop for a minute's rest. She often baked at night when it was cool. Maggie, the other foster child, heated the heavy black pressing iron on the stove, then labored over the pillowcases. The room smelled of scorched cotton and starch.

"I don't hardly know this place," Pa said, frowning.

The farm was transformed. The tables on the porch were covered with tablecloths and set with cruets of oil and vinegar, sugar bowls, and flowers. Maggie was good at finding flowers in the field. Queen Anne's lace, daisies, wild roses, indian paint brush. Harry had started to teach Maggie the piano, but they didn't have any more time.

"Where am I going to keep my pipe?" Pa complained.

"You can't keep matches around when there are children. You'll have to smoke in the barn if you want to own the barn next winter."

She often reminded him that if it weren't for the boarders, they would not have the income to pay those bills.

When she cooked the meals, Harry peeled potatoes, stripped corn, churned butter, and pumped water. His arm hurt and so did his shoulder.

When the boarders were settled, it was even worse. One mother had an infant, and Harry had to pump one thousand strokes for enough water to rinse the diapers. Then he and Maggie had to hang them on the line.

Maurice, the name of the boy Harry's age, was always fighting with his sister, Mona. He teased her, "mona bologna." She screamed back. Then the mother yelled at both of them. The farm began to sound like the foster home he had hated. And the women treated Harry and Maggie like they were servants. "This towel is thin, do you have another?" "Would you get me my sweater?" "I'd love a soda." "Just heat the baby's bottle a little."

Harry wondered who was milking Clementine. He missed the rough camaraderie of the hired men. They were bringing in the first hay, but Ma said that she couldn't spare Harry. Instead of going out at dawn with Pa to the warm musky barn, he had to collect kindling, split wood, and start pumping water for the commodes.

*   *   *

One afternoon, when Barney's Restaurant was emptied of the lunch crowd, Harry was sorting through some old sheet music that Barney said came with the piano. Harry hummed, "Ma, he's making eyes at me," a popular Eddie Cantor song, when he sensed Barney standing beside him.

Harry lifted his head and stared into the eyes of the painted tiger.

Barney muttered, "Get lost for a while."

A policeman and a woman dressed in a felt hat, long suit, and brown leather shoes, had entered the restaurant. They were looking around. The woman stared at the bar.

"Hello, there, officer. Can I help you?" Barney ambled over to them.

As Harry slipped back through the kitchen, he heard the policeman say, "I hear tell you got some young boys working for you."

"I got a cook and a dishwasher working for me, and they ain't seen young in thirty years," Barney answered.

Down in the storeroom, Poke's bedroll lay open on the floor. His blanket was missing.

Harry was frozen for a moment.

Quickly, he shoved aside the cans of tomato soup. The opened can wasn't there, either. The money was gone.

He could hear the tone of the voices from the restaurant upstairs. The policeman's deep voice, the woman's higher one.

TEN

BEFORE HE RAN AWAY, EXCEPT FOR MILK-
ing and chopping wood, Harry's chores on the
farm had changed. He was needed more in the house.

Three meals had to be set up, cooked, served,
and cleared from the tables every day. Ma, anxious
to please, did a lot of cooking. Maggie arranged the
serving platters. The boarders always found something to complain about. "Is this butter fresh? I only
like white meat . . . " which meant running back and
forth to the kitchen.

Pumping water. That was the thing. Harry's arm
and back ached.

He carried in cords of kindling and firewood to
feed the big iron stove.

Between meals, there were always errands.
"Harry, run upstairs and get my scarf before the sun
ruins my hair. Get me a hanky from the top drawer.
I'm chilly, my sweater is in the closet. We need the
playing cards, the citronella . . . "

Even toilet paper for the backhouse. The family
still used squares of newspaper, but the boarders
used toilet paper. Ma doled out a roll a day, but the

boarders always asked for more.

No one asked Maurice to do anything. Not even his own mother. He hung around taunting his sister.

He stole money from his mother's dresser and pointedly asked Maggie if she had seen it when she cleaned that day.

Maggie was shocked and distressed. She was hoping Ma would keep her through the winter. But Ma was tired and overworked. She became more involved with the boarders and more distant from the foster children.

*   *   *

Harry sat on the orange crate in Barney's storeroom. He'd thought Poke was his friend. Friends can disagree; they can leave you behind. But friends don't steal from each other. He should have known not to trust Poke. He'd stolen from Harry the first day he rode the rails.

Harry considered letting himself be caught. At least the State of Connecticut Welfare Department cared enough to send the police and a social worker to search for him. How would he ever find his father, anyway? Chicago was a big city. The address on the last postcard was over a month old. There was no work for his father in California. Maybe he'd left Chicago if he couldn't get a job there. Or maybe he did find work and made new friends. A new life. Maybe he'd forgotten all about his wife and son by now.

A lot of kids in foster care were deserted by their fathers.

Harry wasn't crazy about this wanderer's life. He liked sleeping in a bed. He liked good food. He didn't even dislike school that much. In fact, he had been looking forward to starting high school this fall. There was a school band and free piano lessons.

Maurice had spoiled those plans. And now Poke. You couldn't trust anybody. Harry felt the rage he knew was in him. It burst into flame. He slammed his fist into Poke's bedclothes. He hadn't let Maurice get away with it, and he wouldn't let Poke get away with it. He stuffed his burlap bag with his belongings and stomped out.

Harry saw Poke right away, of course. He sat on the platform holding his overstuffed bag, smiling, right out in the daylight in front of everyone.

With a howl, Harry jumped him. They rolled over and over punching and gasping. Harry was smaller than Poke but his sense of Poke's treachery gave him more strength. He finally pinned the older boy down.

"You're nothing but a thief! A thief!" he yelled into Poke's face.

But Poke was laughing. "And you're nothing but a sucker, Harry," he mocked, laughing.

Harry was taken aback. "What's so funny?"

"You. You'd never leave Barney's. You were happy as a lark there, playing your little tunes and getting all that glory." He mimicked, "What a talented boy. A

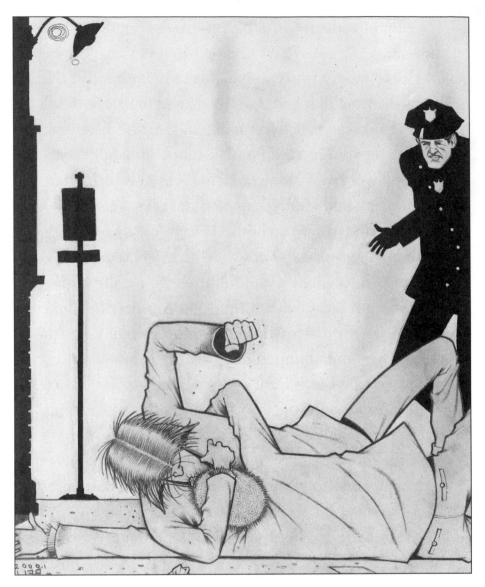

regular Mickey Rooney. So cute, too."

"Shut up," Harry grumbled, getting up and shouldering his pack.

"Now get ready if you're going. The 5477 is rumbling along."

The train's roar blocked everything out. Harry plunged ahead. He heard Poke running behind him.

The freight car reared up like a two-story building. He tossed in his burlap bag, grabbed the door, and hung on.

He wasn't even scared. He was getting good at it. His foot was sure, his arms were strong. He hauled himself into the car, which was filled with blue and white boxes marked spaghetti in red letters.

"Come on, Poke!"

Harry got his footing and looked back. He screamed, "P-o-k-e!"

Poke was being restrained by the policeman. The policeman had his arms around Poke's chest in a strong hold. Poke was kicking.

A woman dressed in brown watched horrified as the blanket opened, and quite a few of Barney's storeroom supplies spilled out on the tracks.

The policeman twisted Poke's arms behind his back. Poke knew he couldn't escape. He stopped struggling.

"C-h-i-c-a-g-o and all points west!" A conductor shouted.

The figures on the platform shrank as the train chugged away.

ELEVEN

CHICAGO. HE MIGHT AS WELL HAVE SAID, I'll meet you in St. Louis. Or Charlottesville, Virginia. Or Baltimore, Maryland. Or heaven, for that matter. Except for the last, Harry was in all of those places. The police knew that Harry was on the train for Chicago. They would have every stop on the way to Chicago watched for Harry. The one place Harry could not go was Chicago.

Poke would never have made it to Chicago anyway. He was probably going to jail for stealing from Barney. Harry learned that trains just didn't go where you wanted them unless you could buy a ticket. If you rode the rails, you just hoped you would get to the one place you were headed. That is, if you were headed any place in particular.

Since Harry didn't care where else he was going besides Chicago, he kept going anywhere.

Most of the time, Harry didn't know where he was. He followed the rest of the bums, down-and-outers who called the rails their home, men with wanderlust, and boys like Poke who went from station to station, freight yard to freight yard, to crosstracks, to sidings.

When he was hungry, he jumped off and went looking for food. Others went door to door begging if they had to. Or they begged at a hobo jungle. Some hoboes, who had lost hope even for adventure, would share watery potato stew or soup, whichever they chose to call it.

Harry hated that part. His father would be ashamed if he knew that his son was begging for food.

Maybe Poke had been right. Maybe when he got too comfortable, Harry didn't want to move. If it weren't for Maurice, he probably wouldn't have run away from the farm, though he'd thought of it before the fight.

Harry had never backed away from a fight, but he didn't look for one, either. He understood how important the boarders were to Ma and Pa Barons' income. A neighbor's farm was foreclosed. At the news, Ma wiped tears from her eyes, and Pa felt helpless and fumed. If it came to a choice, Harry was the one who would be sent away. Harry held back when Maurice tripped the girls, or when he heard him mumbling how much he hated the farm. "This is some ree-sort," he would say. "It stinks." Or when Harry had to wait on the table, he'd whisper. "Where's your apron, Miss?" Or, "Don't expect no tip." Or, "This meat's tough," and he would chew it up and spit it out in front of everyone.

In a funny way, Harry felt sorry for the other boy even though it was Maurice who had everything he wanted, including a doting mother. Maurice couldn't seem to have a good time. He wouldn't go swimming in the pond because he said it was dirty. He cheated at games. He thought playing the piano and singing was "sissy stuff." One day, when they were out picking berries, Harry and Maggie were laughing at their mouths stained blue from tasting the fruit.

"You two look disgusting," said Maurice.

"You'll take that back when you taste Ma's berry pie she promised for tonight," Harry said with enthusiasm.

Maurice, totally bored, said that Ma would never keep her promise, she was a liar.

"What do you mean?"

"She promised me a bedroom her son slept in, but it smells like those barn hands slept in it. She said there was a swimming hole, and it's a mucky pond. And she said there was another kid to play with. But I don't play with the kitchen help."

"Ma's no liar. Take that back!"

"Make me, sissy!"

He pushed Harry. Harry fell back a few steps. Harry grabbed him in an arm lock and brought the other boy down on his back. There were howls of pain.

Pain from Maurice because he fell on a berry bush. Pain from Harry because good people seemed to have it so bad. His mom, his dad, who tried so hard, and Ma, who worked all day and night to please Maurice and his stupid family.

Maurice pretended to be knocked out, but, when Harry loosened his grip, Maurice delivered a surprisingly stunning punch.

He stood over Harry, his face alight. Apparently, fighting was something Maurice liked.

Harry exploded. His fists shot out like windmills. Maurice kicked him. Harry danced around Maurice. Maurice began to breathe hard. Harry dodged the other boy's blows. Maurice's punches were weakening. He was getting tired. Harry jumped on Maurice and knocked him backward. "Take it back!" He pinned the other boy's shoulders down to the ground.

"I . . . I . . . " Maurice sputtered.

Maggie cried, "Don't kill him, Harry, please don't kill him!"

Mona was running home, screaming, "Mama, Mama, he's killing Maurice."

*　　*　　*

Harry shook the memory away and realized that it had been twenty days since he left Bridgeport, and he was still far away from Chicago. Maybe the police had stopped their chase by now.

"Get on a cattle train if you want to go to Chicago," another stowaway advised him.

TWELVE

"THEY'RE SEARCHING THE TRAIN. WE better get off, quick!"

The shocking message ran from one car to the other. Shocking, because the train was speeding through the Illinois countryside.

"Wait for a whistle stop," Harry warned the boy who called himself Flash. He couldn't be much older than Harry, and, if he thought naming himself after Flash Gordon, the comic hero, made him sound tough, he was wrong. He looked scared.

"Don't be afraid," Harry said, confidently. "When the train slows down enough, you'll hear the signal."

When the lights of the tiny crossing showed ahead, the train slowed down. The whistle blew. "Jump!" Harry cried.

The ground sped swiftly beneath Harry. A hard contact. He rolled over holding his arm.

He had jumped alone. Flash was still on the train.

The trainmen were sweeping their flashlights through the cars. Flash would hide behind the barrels marked Safety Gloves, but his fear would make him shake or gasp or just give himself up.

The scared ones were always caught.

No wonder President Roosevelt said, "The only thing we have to fear is fear itself."

*   *   *

After Harry checked himself out for bumps and bruises, he brushed off his clothes. He had landed right on the edge of the town of Hope. A big sign read, "Welcome To Hope, Illinois."

Harry walked a couple of blocks following the trolley tracks. He could hear the merry sound of the bells in the distance. He passed an abandoned auto body shop. Harry peered inside the tavern next to it. Several shadows lined the bar, but there was no sign of a piano.

Harry flattened himself against the building as two shabby men stumbled out. They didn't see him—or much of anything else for that matter. The rumble and clang of a trolley drowned out their argument.

Harry smelled the faint odor of broiling beef. He followed his nose past the theater, which was showing a Tom Mix movie. Tom Mix was Poke's hero. Harry wondered if they ever took kids in reform school to the moving pictures.

The door to a cleaning shop was open. A sign read, "Suits Pressed. Hats Blocked." He could smell the steam from the press, see the presser shaking out a pair of trousers. A row of wooden heads lined the shelf above him like trophies. They were shaping fedoras with wide brims like the gangsters in the newspapers wore, and narrower brims that businessmen liked. There were derbies and two stetsons and one high top hat for show. Guess there were still a few rich men around.

Apparently, the smell of food attracted someone else. A tiny white puppy was struggling to climb the steps of the luncheonette from where the smell came.

"Hello, there, little guy," whispered Harry. He picked it up and held it shivering against his chest. The puppy was young. It chewed Harry's finger.

The luncheonette had a counter and stools. A hand-made menu was posted in the window.

Today's special!!!
2 eggs with bacon, juice, 15 cents
Soup and bread, 5 cents
Hamburger with onions, 5 cents
Free coffee with order.

Harry didn't have one cent, or a scrap of food to feed the puppy. He slid down against the brick wall of the building. He held the puppy, feeling its warmth, the beating of its tiny heart.

"Did someone want to get rid of you, too?" he whispered.

He looked down at himself. The soles were pulled away from his shoes. His clothes were filthy. His arms and legs were scratched. He tried to keep himself clean by washing every time he could find a men's room with a sink. It didn't matter. The coal dust was pasted into his hair and skin. It smudged his face. He smelled of smoke and oil.

Harry felt like he had been riding the trains forever. Even here on a sidewalk, he felt the swaying, the rumbling. His ears rang with the noise. And there was always that little core of fear.

Trainsick, they called it.

He closed his eyes. The puppy stopped chewing and snored softly. Harry slept.

When he woke, there were two nickels and six pennies on his burlap bag.

Pets weren't allowed in stores, especially food stores, but Harry hid the pup inside his jacket and went inside. They ate together on the sidewalk curb. After they shared a hamburger and a container of milk, both felt better.

Harry nuzzled Snowball. "Snowball. That's what you look like." How he wanted to keep this warm living thing that had come to him by chance. Snowball's little hind end wagged every time he looked at Harry. His button eyes glowed with love.

"You like that name, don't you?"

But what was Harry going to do with this dog? Strayed and abandoned animals roamed the streets of the city. People in the city couldn't take care of pets.

He wanted to keep Snowball.

Snowball would be company for Harry when he felt lonesome. Sleeping with Snowball in his arms would keep him warm. He could teach the dog tricks. "I'd have to toss you on the train with the burlap bag just before I jump up myself," he said, looking into Snowball's eyes.

But getting thrown like that might hurt or even kill a puppy.

And when I have to hide, he might just bark and give me away.

And how would he feed Snowball? He could barely feed himself.

Bells clanging, the trolley approached. A sign on the front read, Sweetbriar Drive. That sounded ritzy enough. Harry spent the rest of his change riding out to Sweetbriar Drive with Snowball wriggling inside his jacket.

A woman stared at him. He could tell that she was expecting to have a baby in the near future. Harry's jacket was doing a snake dance as Snowball squirmed. He poked his little head out and licked Harry's chin.

The woman smiled.

Harry got up and changed his seat.

Sometimes you had to think of what was best for someone else. Snowball should have food to eat and a yard to play in.

When the trolley reached a quiet street of white houses and green lawns, Harry got off. Two little girls were bouncing big blue and white balls in their driveway. One swung her leg over the ball to the rhythm of "One, two, three O'lary/I spy Mrs. Sary/sitting on her bumble-ary/ . . . "

"Oh look at that cute doggie," the other girl cried. They both dropped their balls and stared at Snowball, who wagged his whole body with joy.

"He's a darling," said her friend, "Here, doggie, what is your name?"

The first girl cuddled Snowball in her arms. "I think he's hungry. Let's ask Mommy if we can keep him."

"I wonder where he comes from."

"That boy dumped him," said the other. "Hey!" she called after the fleeing Harry.

"Snowball," Harry called back. "His name is Snowball."

*   *   *

Harry caught a free ride on the rear of the trolley and rode back to town. He jumped off at the whistlestop and waited to catch the next train wherever it went.

THIRTEEN

HARRY WAS VERY LUCKY. BY CHANCE, HE caught the right train out of Hope. He found himself in a car along with some crates of live chickens. They cackled and crowed. The odor was overpowering.

When the train stopped at a depot, Harry managed to sneak off and into the men's room. He washed his face and drank some water. He hoped to sneak on again in another car.

Luckily, the passenger and luggage cars were detached from the freight cars. He ran out of the depot and jumped on a freight as it was being uncoupled and attached to another locomotive.

Much more at ease among the bales and barrels, he was not surprised to see someone else sitting on the floor eating a sandwich. The man was wearing a black Derby hat.

"Derby!" Harry cried.

Derby put his finger to his lips and whispered, "Hi, ho, Harry! You still on the road?"

Harry flung his arms around Derby, and Derby clapped Harry on the back. It was so good to find someone who knew him.

*　　*　　*

"Still looking for your old man?" Derby asked softly.

Harry nodded. They didn't dare talk out loud while the train took on its new cargo. They heard the sounds that belonged to a world "out there" where people lived and worked without fear of being seen or heard. It seemed very free to Harry.

"You're on the right train to Chicago," Derby whispered. He had some sandwiches that he said his cousin had packed for him. Harry was hungry, as usual, and these were homemade pot roast sandwiches on white bread.

"But what are you doing here?" Harry asked.

"I'm going to Chicago, too," said Derby. "I got a job."

"Hey, that's swell!" Harry said.

"When I got to New Jersey, I made a telephone call to my sister," Derby said, "My brother-in-law just opened a shoe shine shop and needs help. He's got to pay off that big footrest the customers use. He couldn't go for the train fare, so I'm traveling in my usual style . . . thanks to the railroad companies." He shivered. "Brr, it's cold here though. Not like sleeping on the beach in Virginia. That was nice." He almost sounded as if he would miss train hopping.

Once the train was on its way again, Harry told Derby of his adventures since their first meeting.

"I wonder what happened to the people I first met when I jumped off the train after Poke," Harry said, as they rode along, bobbing to the motion of the car.

He described the "well-dressed" man, the family with little children.

"If the man was well-dressed, he was probably a ruined business man. They don't usually last on the rails. Can't get used to the life. Me, I always been poor, I know how to get along. If you don't have hope, you can't lose it."

"As for the family, plenty of families are getting along better now that the government gives them relief. President Roosevelt has this program, FERA, it's called. They could get about ten dollars a week with kids. Only a lot of people are too proud to take a handout. But it's only till Papa finds work."

They rode for a long time, making several stops. Derby shared his lunch with Harry. Harry found himself telling Derby about how he got into a fight with Maurice and knew that he could not go back to the farm. He told Derby how he hid in the woods and that Maggie, the other foster child, found him and helped him by bringing back his clothes stuffed in an onion bag with another bag of food. And the little money he had saved. She even brought him her allowance.

Derby said, "I'm sure those boarder folk threatened to leave if Ma didn't notify the agency. You can't change what's done anyway. Just think you did good, Harry. You gave Ma a chance to earn her mortgage money."

"Either way, I could have been sent somewhere else," Harry said.

It was late afternoon when Harry sniffed the air and made a face. The chicken train again?

"Whew! what's that smell?"

Derby laughed. "It's a good smell, means we got some cattle cars on this train. And they go to the Chicago stockyards. Want to get off now? Or see the stockyards. May as well. You'll learn something."

The stench from the stockyards wafted miles away from its source. As the train slowly chugged to a stop, Harry and Derby climbed outside and carefully found their way to an end freight car. They stood on the ladder looking out.

A vista of braying animals spread before them. As far as they could see, there were thousands of steers, pigs, lambs . . . .

Men in high rubber boots sloshed through the muck, carrying heavy chutes to lean against the cattle cars. Others on the train herded the cattle down the chutes to the holding pens. Derby explained that the big pens belonged to the giant beef companies, Armour, Swift, Cudahey.

Other men waited at the bottom of the chute, seemingly unaware that tons of brawn and muscle were sliding down on them.

Derby pointed to a man in a Western hat standing in the pen nearest their freight car. "That's the commission agent. He represents the farmer. He deals with the big company buyers." They listened as the men spoke loud to hear each other.

A buyer, in a peaked cap that read "Swift & Co.," prodded a passing animal with his cane. "Whose shipment is this?"

"Farmer Kowalski from Indiana."

"That man knows how to finish cattle. I'll give you half a cent liveweight."

"That's choice at 1,200 pounds," the commission agent shrugged. "Swift can't do better than this for choice. We're asking 3-4 cent per pound."

Harry didn't have to get an "A" in arithmetic to figure out that a 1,200 pound animal would sell for six to eight dollars.

"No wonder Pa keeps milk cows," he said to Derby. "He got two dollars from the cattle dealer in Connecticut for a newborn calf. It costs a lot of money to raise a full-grown cow. Then you have to pay the freight on top of that."

"You know a lot about farming for a city boy," Derby sounded impressed. He sighed, "It's hard to make a living these days."

They hurried away to take deep breaths of fresh air.

*   *   *

After they had walked quite a while, with Harry craning his neck to see the sights, weaving traffic

and pedestrians, in an unending parade of people and vendors, he and Derby came to a stop.

Chicago was like New York the way a vanilla ice cream cone is like a strawberry one. They were both noisy, bustling cities, but each had its own flavor. In New York City, the subway ran underground, but in Chicago, it ran overhead. Derby pointed up to the tracks. "That's the elevated train tracks. Here, they call it the Loop. It runs like the figure eight into the city and back again. Here is where we stop, son. You go your way, and I go another," he sighed.

"I hope the job with your brother-in-law works out," Harry said. He wondered if Derby could stay in one place.

Derby reached inside his shirt. "Time to pay our own fares, Harry boy."

He thrust some coins and a piece of paper into Harry's hand. "If you don't find your father tonight, call me at this number."

Then he took Harry's hand and shook it. "God bless you, son."

Harry wanted to say, "You're a nice man, Derby. And I'm glad I met you," but even before he could say, "Thank you," Derby was gone.

FOURTEEN

IT FELT STRANGE TO HARRY TO PUT MONEY in a turnstile and take a subway seat high up in the air. He imagined flying through the sky in an airplane.

Suddenly, he felt panicky. Not from the flying part, but from the risk of what he was doing. What if his father were furious with him? What if he were out-of-work and had nothing to share with Harry? What if he had already moved on?

A map on the wall displayed the train's route. He checked three stations from the district in which his father lived. Three stops. What if he got out at the wrong station? He was lost and alone in a big, unfriendly city.

He felt in his pocket for the scrap of paper that Derby had given him.

The train and the passengers swayed together. The passengers were startlingly clean. One lady with a child moved away from him. Others stared. He realized that he was not a pretty sight. Or smell.

I rode the rails, and I didn't get caught, he thought. *I was never arrested for vagrancy. I didn't get hurt or beat up. I was lucky. Nothing bad happened to me.*

There were many things that didn't happen to Harry on his journey, but there were many things that did happen.

One thing . . . he met all different sorts of people, all colors, all stations in life. Most of them were nice. Most people had something you could like about them. But you didn't have to like what they did.

He could like the nice part of the boy known as Poke, but he didn't have to like the things Poke did.

Harry had learned the difference.

He felt a deep sadness for Poke. He wished that he could have helped him. Harry wasn't old enough, and there hadn't been time enough to prove to Poke that there were other ways for him to act. Most likely, they'd send Poke to some juvenile home, and Poke would run away again and never get an education. He'd never get out of the "bad boy" character he had to play. Maybe it was too late. Maybe he couldn't get out of it.

Harry wondered if he'd ever see Poke again.

And Derby. Harry really liked Derby. But he didn't want to live like Derby when he was a grown-up. As a kid, he had to prepare himself to be a man. Maybe an engineer on a train. Maybe a lawyer or a doctor.

No one could really take care of you unless you were a baby. You weren't going to do everything people told you to do without asking questions or sometimes saying no. Because that wouldn't be taking care of yourself, either.

Taking care of yourself. Knowing you have to make your own choices. Figuring out what the outcome would be.

He watched the people getting on and off at the station. One more stop. One more stop.

Harry stood up near the door and held on to a pole. He looked down at the streets of Chicago and thought he saw a dog. A little white pup like Snowball.

He wondered what Snowball was doing. In his imagination, he saw Snowball running with a red ball in his mouth. The little girl had thrown the ball. Snowball ran up to her but wouldn't give her the ball. Instead he backed away, teasing her. The little girl ran after him. They were both laughing.

The picture he imagined made Harry laugh, too. He wondered why he had thought of the ball as red.

Harry had done the best he could with Snowball. He had to give the puppy up, but at least, Snowball had a chance to live in a nice home.

Had his dad felt that way about him, too?

*   *   *

Chicago. Hog butcher to the world.

So Carl Sandburg, the American poet Harry had studied in eighth grade English, called the city. It was also "the home of the blues."

Funny. It was as though Chicago was a brawling bully of a city on the outside, but a gentle singing one inside. As Harry walked along the streets looking for the number of his father's rooming house, music meandered from every doorway. But no matter what the beat, Harry's shoes tapped on the sidewalk. Music seemed to rise from his torn soles.

*   *   *

"No," said the frowning man who answered the door. "Mr. Harmony is not home." He peered at Harry in the darkened hallway. "Who are you?"

"I'm his son," Harry said.

"Well, come on in." The man held the door open.

Harry followed him down a long dark corridor. They were directly over a restaurant, and he could smell the cooking. For once, it didn't make him hungry. It was a stale cabbage odor.

"Does your dad expect you?" the man asked, unlocking the door at the end of the hall. He looked at Harry's ripped clothes.

"It's kind of a surprise," said Harry.

The room was furnished with a bed, a dresser, a faded arm chair, and a table, but succeeded only in looking bare. Dad's practice keyboard was on the table with a neat pile of sheet music.

Some letters lay on the dresser. A silver frame held a picture of Harry and his mom. A snapshot of the three of them was stuck in one corner of the mirror.

The man held the snapshot at arm's length.

"It could be you," he said, comparing Harry to the snapshot.

Dad had one tuxedo hanging in the closet with a cleaner's bag over it. A shapeless coat, a shabby suit, several pairs of pants, and a couple of shirts completed his wardrobe.

Not exactly the home of a playboy!

"Whew!" The man said. "The bathroom is down the hall. You better take a shower and put on one of your dad's clean shirts."

Harry felt squeaky clean after the shower. He put on his dad's underwear and socks, and rolled up his trousers.

Alone in the room, he picked up the two letters on the bureau. Harry read his own letter that he'd written his dad. It sounded stupid.

The other letter was from his mother.

"Dear Ben," it read, "Swell news that Harry James is leaving Benny Goodman's band to put his own group together. I hear swing all the time on the radio. I do believe big bands are it now. That means more musicians will have work. Including you, my dearest.

"The doctors say that in a few months, I may be able to leave here. Our boy and I could stay some place in the country . . . is this only a dream?"

Harry stood, still holding the letter. He had always thought of his parents as distant parts of himself. They were there, like your arm or your leg. You didn't think about them until you needed them.

And if your arm was hurt and you couldn't lift anything, or your leg was broken and you couldn't walk, you got awfully upset.

If your parents couldn't function the way you wanted them to, you got upset, too. You got mad at your sore arm and your broken leg and your poor parents.

His parents were poor. His mother was sick. They couldn't make him the home he wanted, or be there when he needed them.

A vision appeared before him. Not the lively young mother in a rose-colored dress. But a stranger lying on a hospital bed, her face too white, her cheeks too red.

A man lived in this crummy room, watching his dreams as a performing pianist fade away. He had not studied at music school just to "tickle the ivories."

Two lovers, lonely for each other, lonely for him, trapped in hard times.

*　　*　　*

There was a loud knock on the door.

The jig is up! Poke would have said. What it meant was that Harry was caught!

The policeman and the lady in brown blocked the doorway, looming over Harry.

"Miss Lane and I were told that you'd be heading

here, young man," said the policeman. "They've been looking for you all over the country."

"Where's my Dad?" Harry asked.

"You caused both your parents and foster parents a lot of worry," Miss Lane scolded.

"To say nothing of your friends and the whole state of Connecticut," the policeman added. "Finding runaways costs money, Harry."

"I didn't think about that," said Harry. "I just didn't want to go to a detention home."

The policeman didn't look so forbidding anymore.

"Whatever happens, Harry, it doesn't help to run away," said Miss Lane. "It's better to stay and face your problems. Your foster family never said a word to the agency about the fight you had with that bully until they had to report that you were missing."

"What will happen to me now?" asked Harry.

"Your dad happens to be playing at the Blue Moon down the street," said the policeman. "We'll take you to him, but remember, you are still a ward of the state of Connecticut."

"Don't worry," Miss Lane said, as they walked single file down the narrow, stuffy hall. "As long as your father is working, he can get you back."

They went out the door to the tough, yet tender, street that lay half in shadow and half in sunshine. Harry walked between the two adults, "Is it okay for me to walk in the sun?" he asked. "I won't run away."

"You go on ahead," said the policeman.

So they let him walk on the sunny side of the street until Harry heard the music and began running toward the Blue Moon.